UGLY ANIMALS

Ugly Sea Creatures

Kerri O'Donnell

PowerKiDS press™

New York

Published in 2007 by The Rosen Publishing Group, Inc.
29 East 21st Street, New York, NY 10010

Book Design: Michael Ruberto

Photo Credits: Cover (left), p. 7 © National Geographic; cover (top right) © Fred Bavendam/Peter Arnold, Inc.; cover (bottom right), pp. 21, 22 © Taxi; p. 3 © Robert Deal/Shutterstock; p. 5 © Bruce Rolff/Shutterstock; p. 9 © Bruce Robison/Corbis; p. 11 © Daniel Gustavsson/Shutterstock; p. 13 © Masa Ushioda/SeaPics.com; p. 15 © Stuart Westmorland/Corbis; p. 17 © Lavigne Herve/Shutterstock; p. 19 © Thomas/Shutterstock.

Library of Congress Cataloging-in-Publication Data

O'Donnell, Kerri, 1972-
  Ugly sea creatures / Kerri O'Donnell.
      p. cm. - (Ugly animals)
  Includes bibliographical references and index.
  ISBN-13: 978-1-4042-3528-0
  ISBN-10: 1-4042-3528-0
  1. Marine animals-Juvenile literature. I. Title.
  QL122.2.O36 2007
  591.77-dc22
                                    2006014624

Manufactured in the United States of America

Contents

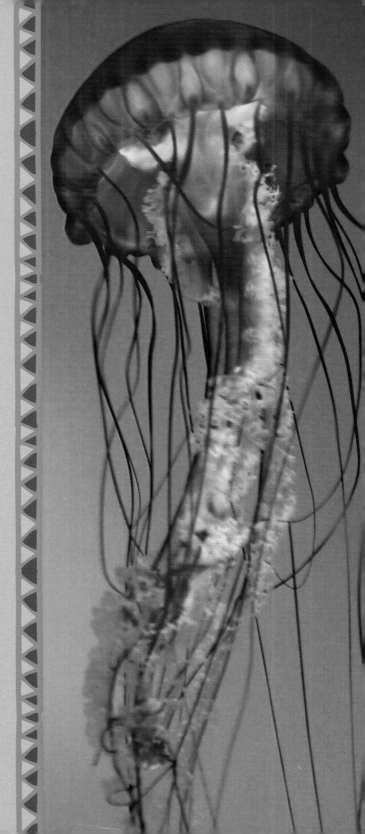

Under the Sea

Have you ever been to the ocean? Maybe you saw fish in the water or a crab in the sand. Most of us only see the ocean animals that live close to the beach. However, scientists think there are millions of kinds of animals living in the ocean!

Some sea animals have beautiful colors and shapes. Others are weird-looking and just plain ugly! Let's look at some of these strange sea creatures.

An aquarium is a good place to see all kinds of sea creatures.

The Viperfish

One of the ugliest deep-sea creatures is the viperfish. The viperfish has a huge mouth filled with razor-sharp teeth. Its teeth are so big that they don't even fit inside the fish's mouth! The viperfish uses its teeth to grab its victims. Its head can flip up so it can swallow large **prey**.

Viperfish live far below the ocean's surface where there is no sunlight. Their bodies make their own light. They use this light to attract prey.

During the day, the viperfish stays about 5,000 feet (1,524 m) below the ocean's surface.

7

The Fangtooth

The fangtooth is another creepy-looking fish that has a big mouth filled with long, sharp teeth. It lives about 16,000 feet (4,877 m) below the ocean's surface. Sunlight doesn't reach that far down, so the water is very cold.

There is not a lot of food where the fangtooth lives. The fish eats anything that floats down from above. This might be why it has such a big mouth—so it can catch other animals' leftovers!

Look at this picture. Can you guess how the fangtooth got its name?

9

The Moray Eel

What fish is long, slimy, and looks like a snake? An eel!

There are about 600 kinds of eels. Eels have long, smooth bodies that can dig into sand or slip between rocks. One kind, the moray eel, is bigger than most eels. Morays are usually about 5 feet (1.5 m) long. That's a big fish! Most fish have scales, but moray eels do not. Their bodies are covered in slimy **mucus**. This keeps them safe from **germs**.

Most moray eels have sharp teeth they use to catch their prey.

The Stingray

A stingray is a fish but looks more like a weird pancake! Stingrays have large, flat bodies and long, thin tails. These tails have sharp **spines** on them that stingrays use to hurt their enemies. The spines hold **poison** and can cause a painful wound.

There are about 100 kinds of stingrays. One kind that lives off the coast of Australia can grow to be 14 feet (4.3 m) long!

Stingrays are related to sharks. Some people call stingrays "pancake sharks."

The Jellyfish

Have you ever seen a fish made of jelly? Jellyfish have something that looks like jelly between their two body layers. This helps them float. Some jellyfish are small. Others are huge! Most have bodies shaped like umbrellas. Arms called **tentacles** hang from their bodies. Jellyfish use these tentacles to sting prey so it can't move. Then they eat it.

Jellyfish can sting people, too. Some stings aren't harmful. Others are very painful. Some jellyfish stings can cause death!

This kind of jellyfish can have tentacles that are 120 feet (36.6 m) long!

The Octopus

People once thought octopuses were monsters because they are so strange-looking. The octopus is a soft, rubbery sea animal with a big head and eight arms covered with cup-shaped suckers. The octopus uses its arms and suckers to move and to catch prey.

Octopuses have many enemies. Sharks, eels, and other animals think the octopus's soft body is a tasty snack! When in danger, an octopus can shoot out a cloud of ink. The ink hides the octopus so it can escape.

If an octopus loses an arm, it can grow another one to replace it!

The Squid

Like the octopus, the squid was once considered a sea monster. Sailors told stories about giant squid pulling men off boats and eating them! That's not true.

A squid looks a lot like an octopus. Its head is surrounded by eight arms and two tentacles it uses to catch prey. The squid then uses its sharp beak to kill its prey. Like an octopus, a squid can shoot out ink to hide it while it escapes from enemies.

Some squid like this one are less than 1 foot (30.5 cm) long. A giant squid can be 60 feet (18.3 m) long!

19

Old and Ugly!

In 1938, a fisherman made a surprising catch off the coast of South Africa. The fish was a coelacanth (SEE-luh-kanth). The first coelacanths probably lived about 400 million years ago. Scientists thought they died off about 65 million years ago, around the same time the dinosaurs did. Now the coelacanth is called a "living **fossil**."

These odd-looking fish can grow to be about 5 feet (1.5 m) long and can weigh about 160 pounds (72.6 kg)!

Coelacanths have bony fins they use like legs to rest on the ocean floor.

Ugly but Cool!

Octopuses and squid can quickly change color to hide from enemies. An octopus can change its skin from smooth to bumpy to blend in with the ocean floor. Moray eels have a great sense of smell they use to hunt for food in dark water. Jellyfish have no brain or heart, but they can live anyway. The coelacanth outlived the dinosaurs.

They might be ugly, but the sea creatures in this book are pretty cool, too!

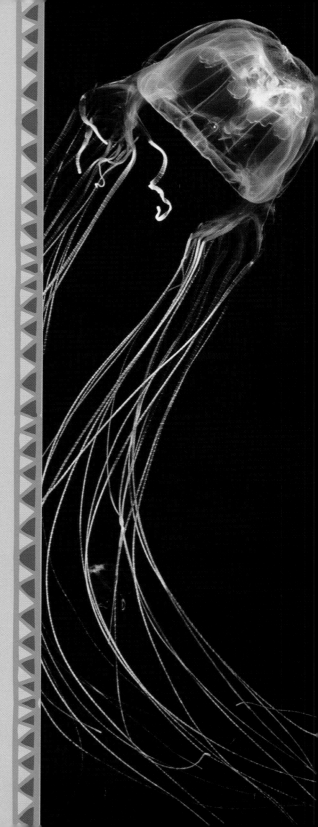

Glossary

fossil (FAH-suhl) The hardened remains of a dead animal or plant that lived long ago.

germ (JURM) A very tiny living thing that can cause sickness.

mucus (MYOO-kuhs) Thick, slimy matter. People have mucus in their nose.

poison (POY-zuhn) Something that can hurt or kill a living thing.

prey (PRAY) An animal that is hunted by another animal as food.

spine (SPYN) A stiff growth with a sharp point.

tentacle (TEHN-tih-kuhl) A long, thin growth on the head or around the mouth of an animal that is used to touch or hold on to something.

Index

A
arms, 14, 16, 18

C
coelacanth(s), 20, 22

D
dinosaurs, 20, 22

E
eel(s), 10, 16
enemies, 12, 16, 18, 22

F
fangtooth, 8
float(s), 8, 14

I
ink, 16, 18

J
jellyfish, 14, 22

L
light, 6
"living fossil," 20

M
moray eel(s), 10, 22
mucus, 10

O
octopus(es), 16, 18, 22

P
poison, 12
prey, 6, 14, 16, 18

S
spines, 12
squid, 18, 22
sting(s), 14
stingray(s), 12
suckers, 16
sunlight, 6, 8

T
teeth, 6, 8
tentacles, 14, 18

V
viperfish, 6

Web Sites

Due to the changing nature of Internet links, PowerKids Press has developed an online list of Web sites related to the subject of this book. This site is updated regularly. Please use this link to access the list:
http://www.powerkidslinks.com/uglyani/uglysea/